TRUE
SISTERS

Praise for *The Liar's Handbook*:

"The best YA novel I've read in ages – gripping and honest. It's a terrific story"   AMANDA CRAIG

"It packs more twists, thrills and topical discussion points into its 125 pages than many full-length novels"   *JEWISH CHRONICLE*

TRUE
SISTERS

KEREN DAVID

Barrington Stoke

First published in 2018 in Great Britain by
Barrington Stoke Ltd
18 Walker Street, Edinburgh, EH3 7LP

www.barringtonstoke.co.uk

A CIP catalogue record for this book is available
from the British Library upon request

ISBN: 978-1-78112-829-9

Printed in China by Leo

For Jesse and Geni

CONTENTS

PROLOGUE / **Clara**

This is how it feels when they raid your house.

It's so early that you're still asleep, and the bang, bang, bang invades your dreams. That's how you hear it first – you're deep in an imaginary forest, hearing the stamping of a giant, the roaring of a bear.

Then you wake up, shocked into the cold room, and the noise doesn't stop. Mama is crying in her room. A long, high wailing cry. You've never heard her cry like that before.

And you don't know if you should run to comfort her or run towards the deafening noise at the door. You make for Mama, but she just screams even louder.

"The door …" you say, and you hear men's voices just outside. There's so much fear bubbling up inside you that you think you're going to be sick. You get halfway down the stairs and then your legs are trembling too much to hold you up, so you sit down. You're hot and cold, and sweat pricks under your armpits and around your hairline. You realise your hair is still loose and you are still wearing your nightdress.

And all the time you hear those voices. Men's voices.

They could be knights or soldiers or giants or goblins. They could be good wizards or bad, bad, bad. They might be the Forces of Darkness. They shouldn't be shouting. But they are.

"Open up!" they shout.

"Police!" they shout.

"Open up!"

And then they all fall silent, and you breathe in and out, and all you can hear is Mama's wails.

Then you look at the door and you can see the piece of wood that Mama nailed over the hole. The hole where papers used to come. Mama said they were bad papers, evil papers.

Anna used to collect those papers. She showed me once. They had pictures of food, with "Take Away" written on them. Then she left.

Mama said Anna had been taken away herself, by the bad spirits in the night.

Then Mama nailed the wood over the hole in the door, and since then the house is quiet and cold and dark. Anna never came back. She said she would, but she didn't.

Now the wood jiggles and jiggles and the men's voices are whispers. Mama's crying turns into a long string of words. One word. "No-no-no-no-no-no-no." And on and on and on. She doesn't stop, even when the piece of wood clatters onto the floor.

You're so scared that you feel the sour acid taste of bile in your mouth. You swallow it back. You have to be strong for Mama.

And then a woman speaks into the hole in the door.

"Clara?" she says. "Clara? Can you hear me?"

You are quieter than a tiny mouse all alone in its dark house after midnight. A mouse with no family and no friends and no town and no country. A lone mouse. A silent mouse.

After Mama stopped talking, Anna was the only one who called you Clara. But that's not Anna's voice.

"We're not going to hurt you," the woman says. "We just want to talk to you. Will you open the door?"

You nearly do. The woman sounds kind. Her voice is soft and gentle, like Mama's voice.

And to tell the truth, you are very curious to see what is on the other side of the door. "Very" isn't the right word, but there probably isn't a word to describe how much you want to know about the world. That desire eats you up, like a worm in the brain. It's such a strong feeling, creeping and eating, intense and over-powering and bad.

So very bad.

Then the woman says, "Anna's talked to us, Clara. We're here to help you. Please open the door."

And you know what to do.

You shuffle forward, one step at a time. Slowly, slowly does it. All the time the woman is talking to you: "That's it. Don't be scared. You can do it. Good girl."

At the bottom of the stairs, you start creeping towards the door. You've imagined it so many times. In your dreams and out of your dreams. Inch by inch. Step by step. Every monster you've ever thought of is waiting for you.

"All you have to do is open the door," says the woman with the gentle voice.

She's watching you. Her eyes are right by the hole. Big brown eyes with lines painted around the lids. You've never seen eyes like that.

You look right into those eyes. You hear her start to talk again. "Anna told us," the woman starts.

But then you grab the piece of wood from the floor where it fell and you shove it into the hole at her. You're so fast that the woman cries out in pain. And when you look again, those eyes are gone.

And you're looking outside at a big tangle of things. Men and cars and trees and people. And you hear the words "Stand back!"

But you stay right where you are.

So when the door crashes in, it hits you in the face. All you can see is blood on your hands and blood pouring down your white nightdress. And there's a man in your house, and he's talking, talking, talking.

You can't hear a word.

You can see men coming in the house, and Mama is screaming and so are you. The men are everywhere with their dirty feet and their dirty hands and their smell and their noise.

Then the woman with the big brown eyes puts her arm around you. She tries to put a cloth to your nose, but you bite her hand.

"Clara," the woman says, "Clara, stop that. You have to come with us."

"I can't," you say. "I can't!"

Then the woman says "Anna" again, and you try to bite again. But she's ready for you this time, and somehow you're held by two of them, your arms gripped tight. However much you struggle, they won't let you go.

Then you step outside.

And there's a small part of you that's seeing everything. Trees – tall and proud and shimmering in the breeze. Flowers – white and purple, and a soft, drooping pink rose that you think must smell like perfume.

But most of you isn't smelling the roses or looking at the trees. Most of you is fighting and crying and screaming for Mama, and hiding under your hair so that you won't see anyone looking at you.

Not the men in dark clothes.

Not the women in trousers, like a man's clothes.

Not the group of five people on the road, some of whom are holding up rectangular bits of metal and pointing them at you. Magical instruments, you think. They are casting spells to take you away.

Then the two women pull you along, and you're right outside the house. You're cold all over, and the ground is hard under your feet. Your heart is pounding so hard it's like a bass drum that's leading soldiers to war.

And then you hear Mama screaming inside the house.

"Mama!" you shout. The people watching make gasping noises, and the two women get you to a car. Anna told you about cars – she told you they were like small houses on wheels that took you away faster than anyone could run after you. One of the car doors is open, and you're panicking, you can't breathe. Then someone pushes your head, pushes your back, and you go from outside to inside.

Inside the car.

And there's part of you that wants to know what it's like to go in a car, wants it so much. You have thought about it so often and now it's happening. And it was Anna, bad Anna, who put this thought in your head.

But you didn't think it would be like this, with a noise that is high and shrill, and a flickering blue light. You're going faster and faster, and you close your eyes tight, because surely no one can travel this fast and survive it.

"It's OK, Clara," one of the women next to you says. "It's OK, darling. Everything's going to be OK."

But you're feeling sick, so sick, moving so fast. This time you can't hold it, so you cough up a bit of yesterday's supper, and it lands on the seat and on her trousers.

"What was that for?" she says.

You gasp, "So fast!"

And the woman in the front says, "We're only doing twenty."

"Clara, listen to me," the woman with the brown eyes says, once she's finished wiping her clothes. "My name is Priti, and I am your social worker.

"We're taking you to a safe place. Somewhere where you can stay for a bit. And then the police will want to talk to you, and so will I. You'll be able to see your mother in a while. And your sister Anna as well. I don't know what the future will bring, but don't be scared. We are here to look after you."

You don't reply. You look out of the window. You spent all those years wondering what the world outside looks like, and it turns out that it's grey and ugly and full of rain.

And that's what it's like when they raid your house.

CHAPTER 1 / **Ruby**

No show

Unbelievable.

It's only the most important day of my life so far. Performance day for my school drama group. All the parents are here, plus assorted grandparents, brothers, sisters, friends. But not my mum.

Dad's here. My stepmum, Kelly. My half-sister, Freya, is asleep in her buggy. She might be asleep, but at least she's present!

Even Adam is here – Kelly's son. He must have a day off from his hairdressing apprenticeship – you'd think he was running that salon if you heard Kelly boasting about it, not just washing people's hair and sweeping up. I'm a bit nervous, seeing Adam here, because he's the funniest person I know but not always the kindest. If he sees a chance for a joke, he just goes for it, and never really thinks about the other person's feelings.

For example, he thinks it's hilarious to call my mum Mother Teresa, after the woman who ran an orphanage in India. I don't think that's very funny. But I never say so.

Anyway, Adam won't find anything to laugh at today. We've rehearsed and rehearsed. I am full of words, full of emotions, ready to change from one character to another. The way I see acting, it's like giving yourself to someone else for a short time. It's like giving them a home and a voice and an audience. And I get a break from being me, which – at times – is a relief.

But where is Mum? Why isn't she here? She *promised*.

"That's enough peeking at the audience," Ms Okafor, our drama teacher, says to me. "Are you ready, Ruby? Not too nervous?"

"I'm fine," I say.

She knows me better than that.

"Do your breathing exercises," Ms Okafor says. "Remember how well the last rehearsal went."

Ms Okafor is the youngest teacher I have and also the best. Sometimes I think she's more like a big sister than a teacher. Sometimes I imagine that she really is my sister, and we can hang out and go to plays and have long chats about stuff. Like she could give me tips about hair, for example. Hers is done in beautiful braids. Mine is more of a frizzy mess.

"I'm fine," I repeat.

"Well, can you check on Milly then?" Ms Okafor asks. "Last time I saw her, she'd turned green in the face and was heading for the loo."

It's a relief to have someone else to focus on.

I find Milly in tears in the Vulnerable Toilet (she has a key because of her anxiety issues). I make her drink some water and suck a mint (I always have them in my bag). Then I dab some Rescue Remedy on her wrist and get her to sniff it, taking deep breaths. Mum's a big believer in Rescue Remedy. She says it works miracles.

Milly calms down a bit and stops crying. Her huge blue eyes are pinkish, and so is her nose, so I pull out my make-up bag and re-do her make-up. "There you go," I say, in my most encouraging voice. "Stunning."

Milly *is* stunning. She has the sort of red hair that looks like autumn leaves. Her eyes are massive, like a baby racoon's, and she's tall and impressive and you can imagine her as anything – a princess in a fantasy film, a rock star, a champion sports star. I spend a fair bit of time wishing I looked as good as Milly. Instead, I have freckles and frizz and I'm short and curvy, which means that some people think I'm fat when actually I'm just normal.

"You're stunning too," Milly says. She lies, but she's my friend, so it's OK. It's more than OK. "You're brilliant, Ruby. Can I have some more of that stuff?"

I dab more Rescue Remedy on her wrist.

"We need to go," I say. "You can do this, Mills."

She squeezes my hand. "So can you."

I don't know if I can. I feel all funny inside. And what if Mum still isn't here? What if she's had an accident or something?

"Your parents are in the front row," I tell Milly.

She pulls a face and says, "I told them not to! Sit at the back, I said. Be there, but not in my face."

I'd love to have Mum sitting in the front row. I'd love to have her there, giving me her total attention. Just for once.

"We can do this," I say. It's more for me than for Milly, who is sniffing her wrist and checking herself in the mirror.

There's a thumping at the door and a voice calls, "Come on, you two! They're all waiting for you! What are you doing in there?"

We open the door. It's Lena. Yuck.

"It's OK ... I was just re-doing Milly's make-up," I explain as Milly locks the door to the Vulnerable Toilet.

"Yeah, right, I totally believe you," Lena says. She manages to make anything sound dirty.

She's always repeating things that people say – pretty normal things – with a wink and a dirty laugh and a nudge in your ribs. She's exhausting.

"Come on," Milly says, and we run to the theatre. Ms Okafor is looking a bit stressed. I feel bad.

"Everyone OK?" Ms Okafor asks.

I'm desperate to look out at the audience again, to see if Mum's arrived. Probably she has. Probably she was just caught up in traffic. Probably she's there, sitting with Dad and Kelly and Adam, maybe bouncing Freya on her knee. For divorced parents, Mum and Dad have the best relationship of any family I know. Some people's parents can't even be in the same room after they split. But that won't be why Mum's not here today.

And it's not that Mum doesn't care. I know she wants to be here.

No, if Mum's not here, it'll be because a new brother or sister has arrived out of the blue.

And I know I shouldn't resent that.

But, to tell the truth, I do.

CHAPTER 2 / **Ruby**

My new sister

After the performance, Dad insists on giving me a lift home. It turns out that Mum had texted me to say she might be held up at home – she never remembers that we have to keep our phones switched off at school. Then she rang Dad just in case, explaining that we were expecting a new arrival that night and she had to get everything ready.

Great.

But then I start wondering who it's going to be, and where they'll have come from. I feel guilty and excited and curious all at once.

Kelly sits in the front with Dad, and I'm jammed in the back, squashed between Freya's car seat and Adam.

"You were wonderful," Kelly tells me for the millionth time. "Wasn't she great, Adam? You're really talented."

"Really great," Adam says. "Like, you could be on reality TV one day."

"*What?*" I say, feeling horrified. "I want to be an actress! Not some awful Z-list celebrity!"

Adam smirks, and I realise he's just teasing me.

"And wasn't your friend lovely?" Kelly continues. "So pretty. Is she trying for Performance Academy as well?"

Just the name gives me a funny feeling in my tummy. Performance Academy is *the* school. The one and only state school in our area that specialises in drama and music and dance. Loads of really big names started out there. Milly and I have both got auditions. Six weeks to go. I can hardly bear to think about it.

"Yes, she is," I say. My biggest fear is that Milly gets in and I don't. I mean, I'd be very happy for her, of course I would, but her success would sort of magnify my own failure. Also, I'd hate it if I got in and she didn't. But that'd never happen.

"Here we are," Dad says as he pulls up outside our house. "See you Saturday, Ruby love."

"See you," I say, and I wave as they drive off. It's been five years since my parents split up, which is a lifetime really. I love Kelly and Freya, and deep down Adam's OK … It's just that sometimes there's something a bit sad about having to say goodbye to Dad at the front gate.

I push open the front door and stroke Wilbur, our cat, who's come to find me. He was a rescue cat, of course. He used to spit and hiss if anyone came near him, but now he lets me pick him up, and he loves it when you tickle him under his chin.

I hear voices in the kitchen. So, whoever it is has arrived already. Mum must have had an emergency call.

"Hey!" I shout. "I'm home!"

Wilbur rushes upstairs. I know where he'll be heading – to his very own laundry basket, which we keep on the landing, full of old towels.

Mum appears at the kitchen door. "I'm sorry, darling!" she tells me. "I'm so upset that I missed it. How did it go?"

"OK, I think." I'm not going to hold a grudge, but I don't want her to think that I'm fine with her no-show. "Milly was really nervous beforehand, so I gave her some of my Rescue Remedy."

"Well done!" Mum says. "And your teacher – Miss Okafell? What did she say?"

"It's Ms Okafor," I say. "It's a Nigerian name. And she said I did very well." I lower my voice to ask, "Who is it? Are they here yet?"

"Come and meet Clara!" Mum says. I spot a tiny grimace cross her face, which I know from experience means my latest foster sibling is going to be tricky.

Maybe Clara will be like Della, who stole everything that wasn't nailed down.

Maybe she'll be more like Lizzie, who spat and swore, and cried and cried and cried every night.

Or maybe she'll be like Jamie, who didn't speak at all. He just sat on the sofa like a ghost, staring at the telly, his eyes hardly blinking, losing himself in other people's stories.

But it'll be all right. We've seen everything over the years. And things normally get better. Mum prides herself on helping all her foster kids. "There's no such thing as a bad child," Mum always says. "Just one that's been treated badly." I thought it was something she'd made up until I heard someone say it on the radio. Except they were talking about dogs.

I follow Mum into the kitchen. It's bigger than you'd expect from looking at the front of the house, because they built an extension before Dad moved out. It's a lovely light room, with sofas on one wall and a big kitchen table. And there's a girl sitting there.

I'd been expecting someone young – because most of the tricky kids have been younger – but this girl is about my age. She's very pale, and her hair is pulled back into two pigtails, stretched tightly back from her forehead. She's wearing tracksuit bottoms and a shapeless black T-shirt. Apart from the clothes, she looks like …

I don't know ... someone from Victorian times? A housemaid from *Downton Abbey*? Her hands are pink and raw, and as I get closer I see that her lips are cracked and bleeding, and her nails look painfully short. She's not wearing a scrap of make-up, and her heavy eyebrows almost meet each other just above her nose. And there's a faint shadow of a moustache on her upper lip. I don't want to judge, but this girl clearly doesn't take many selfies.

In a way, I admire her for that. But she'd really stick out at school.

Clara oozes tension. She doesn't need to say anything, it just seems to surround her like an invisible cloud.

I can almost hear Ms Okafor's voice in my ear: *How does she give you that feeling? What can you copy as an actress?* I see that she has hunched her back. Her face has a pinched frown. Her hands twitch on the table.

"How about I put the kettle on?" Mum says.

I put a huge smile on my face and sit down at the table with her. "Hi, Clara!" I say. "I'm Ruby. Welcome to our family!"

Clara doesn't smile at all. She's staring at something just behind me. I turn around, but I can't see anything there. Maybe Wilbur is lurking in a corner. That's the thing about black cats – they're very good at hiding.

"Hey, we should make a cake!" I say. "We always make a cake for new arrivals."

It can be a good way to break the ice, if we do something together. But then, most of the kids we foster are under eleven. Cake is an easy win. Clara doesn't even crack a smile. Never mind. I start getting out ingredients. Flour. Sugar. Butter. Eggs.

Clara gets to her feet. "I don't want your cake," she says.

"You probably need a rest," says Mum. "Why don't I show you your room, and then you can come down and have something to eat later?"

Clara's hands squeeze into fists, and her mouth purses. There's something about her eyes that makes me think she's about to cry. But she doesn't shed a tear. Instead, Clara says to Mum, "I don't want your food. I don't like you or the girl. I don't want to be here. Can you arrange for me to leave?"

CHAPTER 3 / Ruby

Nothing but a liar

Clara marches out of the kitchen and sits on the floor by the front door. She puts her head against the letter box. She must be freezing – a massive draught whooshes in under that door.

Mum and I have the most awkward supper, speaking in whispers so Clara won't hear.

"Oh my god, Mum," I say. "She's a nightmare!"

"Shhh, Ruby, that's not fair," Mum tells me. "We don't know what's happened to her."

"She's totally rude and unfriendly!"

"She's just telling it as she sees it," Mum says. "She doesn't understand why she's here, and she wants to go home. It's only natural."

I pause to fork a fish finger, then ask, "Why is she here?"

"All I know is that there was a raid on her home this morning and social workers removed Clara and her mum. Her mum's in hospital. The social worker says she may have been abused. Clara has an older sister who she's going to see soon. Maybe she'll go and live with her."

"Is her mum ill?" I ask.

"I think it's more of a mental illness."

I start feeling a tiny bit more sorry for Clara, partly because I hope she'll be off to live with her sister very soon. Or maybe Clara could go and live with her mum in a refuge or something, when her mum is feeling better. And then I think a bit about the sort of abuse that Clara might have suffered, maybe from a dad or her mum's boyfriend. She must have been very scared. She must have been terrified.

"Shall I go and offer her some chips?" I say.

"I'll do it," Mum replies. She closes the door behind her, and all I can hear is her soft voice murmuring to Clara.

And then Clara's voice comes loud and clear: "No. I don't want your food. Go away. Leave me alone."

Mum comes back. "Oh dear. Maybe we'll try her with cake. She does look hungry, poor little scrap."

"She should just have something to eat then," I say. My cake is ready, and I take it out of the oven. It's a banana cake – they're really easy. It's golden brown and smells so sweet that I'm sure Clara won't be able to resist it.

"Let it cool down," says Mum, "and then we'll give her a slice. She must be feeling overwhelmed. Remember Jamie?"

Jamie cried for three days solid when he arrived. But after that, he ate, he slept and he did seem to like Mum and me, even if he didn't say very much. And at school he tried hard with his reading and ... *What about school?* I think.

"Mum, where does Clara go to school?"

"Ah," Mum says. "This is the thing. She hasn't been going to school at all, as far as Priti knows. That's her social worker."

I nod and say, "I remember Priti. She was Hassan's social worker too."

"Yes," Mum replies, and her face brightens up at the mention of Hassan. He was great. He was seventeen and had come here from Syria. All he wanted was to learn English and fit in and be part of our family. He used to cook us Syrian food and teach me Arabic. We all cried when he got his refugee status and could go to Manchester to live with his uncle.

"Hassan came to my school," I say. "Is Clara ...?"

"I think she will," Mum replies. "Priti says they have a place in the right year. I'm going to ring the school's family-liaison officer tomorrow."

"But ... how old is she?" I ask. I'm praying that Clara will be younger than me. Or older. Just not the same age. Just not in my year. In my mind I curse Luca Morelli from my tutor group – he left last week to go back to Italy with his family.

"I think Clara's about fifteen or sixteen," Mum says. "I'm sorry, Ruby, but it will help her if you take her in – if you can buddy her a bit."

"Great," I say. "Superb. That's going to be easy."

Mum cuts a piece of cake and puts it on a plate. She pours milk into a glass.

"We're so lucky," Mum says, "and other people aren't."

I'm not sure that we're so lucky. It's not like we're super rich or anything. Is it lucky to be normal?

"Come and help me talk to Clara," Mum says.

We go out into the hallway. It's freezing. Clara is even paler than before.

"Come on upstairs, Clara," Mum says. "It's late now. You're not going anywhere tonight."

Clara blinks at Mum. I can see Clara's tired – her head is beginning to droop.

"You've got the best room," I tell her. "Come and see."

She opens her mouth and then closes it again. She struggles to her feet. She's staring at the milk and cake.

"If I stay here tonight, can I see Mama tomorrow?" Clara says. Her voice is less angry and aggressive now. In fact, she sounds wobbly and full of tears, and I feel sorry for her.

"You come upstairs and have a snack and a sleep," Mum says. "Then in the morning we'll ring Priti and find out what's happening with your mother. Is that OK? Come on now, follow me."

We troop up the stairs – first Mum, then Clara and then me. Mum leads the way to the room right at the end of the landing. I see Clara's eyes widen when she sees the soft green carpet, the dark-green duvet cover and pillows, the fluffy cream blanket.

"I've put some spare clothes in the chest of drawers and wardrobe for you," Mum says. Mum never throws anything out. All my old clothes – and anything that our foster kids grow out of – are all washed and folded and packed away until someone needs them.

Clara sits on the bed and drinks her milk and eats the cake (but without saying thank you or anything like that). Her face looks pinker and a bit less pinched and tense.

"I hope you're comfortable," Mum says. "And maybe you can see your mum tomorrow. Or perhaps your sister."

Clara stares. She slams the glass down on the bedside table.

"I'm not seeing Anna," Clara says. "She isn't my sister any more. She's nothing but a liar, and I never want to speak to her again."

CHAPTER 4 / **Clara**

The witch's house

They have taken me to a witch's house.

Her name is Lydia, and she wears black clothes, and her hair is long and dark. She has a black cat, and her daughter – she calls her Ruby – has dark skin, like someone from a far-off land.

Her tricks and spells are all around. Food that is sweet and smells good and makes me sleep. A magic box of moving pictures. Soft cushions and hot water and perfumes that smell so good that they must be magical – they cannot be real.

The stealer, Priti, came to the house again, with two more women – police officers, they said.

They asked so many questions.

Did Mama hurt me?

Did Mama let me out of the house?

What did we eat?

What did I learn?

Was I scared of Mama?

When did I last see Anna?

I didn't answer, but I kept on asking them my questions.

When can I see Mama?

Is she all right?

Why won't they let me see her?

And in the end the women went away, and I was left with the witch.

And she said, "You can trust me, Clara. No one's going to hurt you. You're safe now."

And then she made me some enchanted soup – chicken soup, she said, with carrots and noodles – and it filled me up and made me sleep.

How can I trust anyone?

CHAPTER 5 / Ruby

Space problems

All in all, it's a relief when we get to the weekend and I go off to Dad's.

I don't always feel like this. Since Freya was born, it's been a bit squashed at Dad's, and sometimes I don't stay over. Instead, Dad and I just spend Saturday together. It wasn't so awkward when Adam used to go off and spend time with his dad, but that seems to have stopped.

So there are more of us in less space. That's why it's not ideal. But no one ever mentions that if Mum didn't need spare bedrooms for foster kids, then she and Dad could have sold the house – our four-bedroomed house with the huge kitchen. Then she and I would probably be in a two-bedroom flat, and Dad would have the money for something bigger.

No one ever mentions it apart from Adam, sometimes. And that's totally unfair, because it's his fault that Mum and Dad got divorced in the first place.

OK, not his fault. Not really. But if it wasn't for him, Dad and Kelly never would have met. Dad had a job as a counsellor in a big school in London, and Adam was being bullied. That's how Dad met Kelly – when he was counselling Adam. And when they got together, that's why Dad lost his job, because he wasn't meant to date the parent of a pupil. It was all super messy for a bit. But we don't talk about it any more.

Anyway, everyone seems to think it's a great idea for me to stay over this weekend. Dad says he hasn't seen me much over the last few months. Mum says perhaps Clara will relax more if it's just the two of them there for the weekend. Kelly texts me to say there's a surprise for me when I get there.

And it is a massive surprise, because they've painted my bedroom pink and put in bunk beds.

"What do you think, eh?" Dad asks me. "I remember you always wanted bunk beds."

"Well, yeah, when I was a bit younger ..." My voice trails off.

"We thought you wouldn't mind for a bit ..." Dad explains. "We need to move Freya to a proper bed and out of our room ..."

"Of course I don't mind!" What else can I say? "And it's a lovely pink."

"Of course, one day Adam will want a place of his own, and then Freya can have his room," Kelly says. "It's just that right now we have space problems."

"It's fine," I tell her. "Honestly! I love bunk beds! And it'll be fun sharing with Freya when she's a bit older."

I'm not going to be able to sleep up there, I know it. Not if Freya's below me and I'm worrying about falling out of bed in the night. But Dad assures me that she's in the cot in their room for now, and it's still my room. My stuff is still in the chest of drawers. But for how long?

Anyway, he and Kelly are off to B&Q, and they ask if I want to go too. But I have homework to do, so I say no, settle myself at the kitchen table with my Maths book and get to work.

About ten minutes later, Adam walks in. I blink. Since last week, he's dyed his hair green.

"Hey," Adam says, and helps himself to a Pepsi from the fridge. "How's it going? Like your new bedroom?"

"I could have done with a warning."

"They wanted to surprise you," Adam tells me.

"Oh well, they did that," I say. "It'll be OK."

"It's not like you're here much anyway," Adam agrees.

I look down at my Maths book and hope he's going to buzz off. Instead, he starts cracking eggs into a bowl, taking care to separate the yolks and whites.

"What are you doing?" I ask.

"I'm making myself an egg-white omelette," Adam replies.

"What even is an egg-white omelette?"

"Everyone has them in Hollywood," he says. "I'm amazed you don't know that. But once you go there you'll find out."

"What do you mean when I go there?" I ask, falling into his trap. "Oh hang on ... ha ha, very funny."

"Ruby, you are going to be a star!" Adam tells me. "It's obvious! Just take me along as your stylist, won't you?"

"Yeah, yeah, right," I say.

"I'd start by straightening your hair ... there's a brilliant thing we do from Brazil."

"I don't need you to straighten my hair. Haven't you heard of #don't touch my hair?"

"Um, no," Adam admits.

I sit up and explain, "Black women like me, we are proud of our natural hair. We don't want people dissing it or touching it or suggesting that we straighten it."

"But you're only half black," Adam points out. "And I'm a hairdresser. I touch everyone's hair."

"You're just the sweeper-up," I say. "And I am a Woman of Colour."

"A Woman of Freckles more like," Adam says. "And, yes, I'm sweeping up now, but you wait."

That's when I have my brilliant idea. "Look, I need your help."

"With your hair?" Adam asks. "Or your style in general? At last! Well, I think we'll have to throw out all of your clothes. You have no idea what suits you."

"No, not me," I say, and make a face at him. "Clara. My new foster sister. She's really weird. And I just think she needs some help to look more ... well ... normal. And then she'll fit in better at school."

"I don't really follow your logic, Ruby," Adam says. "And I'm not such an expert at fitting in in schools. Or looking normal." He says "normal" like he'd say "maggots" or "bigots" or "vomit".

Ouch. That was a stupid thing for me to say. When Adam came to my school, he spent half his time in the art room and the rest of it in the Vulnerable Toilet. It was because of Adam that the school now has a policy on homophobia. It sounds good but really just confirms that the school wasn't the safest of places to be LGBT+, and in my opinion it still isn't. It's not something I would want to test, anyway.

"Adam ..." I begin, but I can't think what to say that won't make things worse.

Adam's got a "don't pursue this or I'll be mean to you" look on his face. So I don't, even if sometimes I want to tell him what Mum says to me: "Your own troubles don't seem so bad if you spend time helping other people with their problems."

Instead, I turn the conversation back to Clara.

"She's got long hair in two plaits, with a centre parting," I tell Adam. "And her eyebrows are really heavy ... almost a monobrow. She's got some dark hair on her face ..."

"Sounds very Frida Kahlo," Adam says.

I have no idea who he's talking about, and say so. So he shows me on his phone. Frida Kahlo was a Mexican artist, and she painted a lot of self-portraits. And she does look quite a lot like Clara, with her heavy black brows – except that Frida Kahlo did more interesting things with her hair, sometimes with flowers. Plus she had really nice earrings and she also wore make-up.

Frida looks very serious and frowny in lots of her pictures, so that's like Clara too. And in some of them she seemed to have a very dark shadow on her upper lip. "Clara does look a bit like that," I say, and hand Adam his phone back.

"I love Frida's moustache," he replies. "It's so fearless and out there and gender neutral and sexy, don't you think?"

"I think she'd look sexier without it," I say, and then feel my face getting hot.

"So Frida's your type?" Adam asks.

"Shut up!" I tell him. "So, what can I do about Clara?"

"Bring her to the salon?" Adam suggests. "It's model night on Monday. I'd love to style a Frida Kahlo."

"She won't come." I know this because Clara refuses to leave the house. She says she's waiting for Priti to take her to her mother. That hasn't happened yet, even though Clara's been with us for four days. I assume it's because her mum is still too ill. "And anyway, they don't let you do styling yet," I add.

"I know. It's so boring. But I could come round to your house and do a makeover?"

"Oh, Adam! That's a great idea! But you have to be nice to her."

"Course I'd be nice to her. When am I not nice? Tuesday?"

CHAPTER 6 / Ruby

She is fierce

Clara loves the television. She's glued to it, Mum says. She doesn't really seem to care what she's watching – anything from Peppa Pig to rugby union. "You'll get square eyes," Mum says, joking, and Clara puts her hands to her face as though she believes her.

Clara has started to eat now too. Tiny mouse portions, eaten in very slow nibbles. Three chips, five peas, one sausage. Mum says it's a start. I wonder if she's got an eating disorder.

And she's starting at my school next week. Mum went shopping last week and bought shoes and underwear, a school bag and gym shoes. Everything else for school is second-hand from me. Mum also bought leggings and hoodies for her, plus jeans and T-shirts. So, Clara looks more normal, but still sort of odd and definitely not as pretty as she could. I offered to show her how to put on make-up, but she said no. Not "No, thank you", just "No".

"It seems silly having to wear uniform for just a few months," Mum says to her. "You'll be doing exams in the summer – well, hopefully, wherever you are."

Clara looks at Mum with those big scared eyes. "I need to go home. I need to look after Mama. I don't want to be here with you."

"I know, sweetheart," Mum says. "But your mama isn't well, and you're going to have to talk to the police and social services. But one day you'll go back to your mum – or to some other form of care. Long-term foster care, perhaps, or a children's home. Try not to worry about it – Priti will make sure you're in the very best place."

"Or they might just let you live on your own," I say, because that's what happened to Leo who lived with us for a bit. His dad threw him out when Leo told his family he was gay. And when he turned seventeen, social services put him in a hostel. He used to come to us for Christmas Day every year, but now he's all grown up and has a husband and a baby, and they've moved to Spain. But he still sends me Christmas cards.

I was only ten when Leo lived with us. It was the first time I realised that sometimes parents could be truly horrible to their children, just because they told the truth about who they were and who they loved. At least I know Mum and Dad will always love me.

Anyway, Clara doesn't say anything, and Mum rushes in with, "I don't think that's very likely, Ruby."

"Where were you at school before?" I ask, but Clara just turns back to the television.

Mum changes the subject. "Didn't you say Milly was coming round tonight?"

"Yes," I say. "I thought it'd be good for Clara to know more people before she starts school." And then I add, casually, "Adam said he'd come over too, to give us a makeover. It's good practice for him at the salon."

Mum looks dubious. "Are you sure?" she asks. "Has he had any proper training yet?" But then the doorbell goes, and it's Milly, and I have to face the reality of introducing her to Clara.

Luckily, Clara's not outright rude, just very quiet. Her eyes keep wandering back to the telly (*Emmerdale*, snore snore) until I grab the remote control and switch it off.

I've told Milly to be ready for Clara's weirdness. "Are you looking forward to coming to our school?" Milly asks. "What's your favourite subject?" She has a big, wide, kind smile that doesn't judge. I love Milly. She's the best friend I've ever had. In fact, I've never really had a best friend before. I always had lots of non-best friends, which Mum says is the best way. But Milly and I both love drama, and we've got so many things in common, and this year we've just spent loads of time together.

"No, I'm not looking forward to school," Clara says. "I don't have a favourite subject. I don't want to go to school."

"It's good to learn," Mum says. "You need an education."

"I'm learning from this." Clara points a bony finger at the television. "This magic picture show. Can you put it on again?"

I glance at Milly and think, *See, I told you she was weird.* But Milly just laughs and says, "Yeah, it is pretty magic. But not *Emmerdale* ... that's just for my nana."

Clara frowns, and I hurry in with, "She means her grandmother," because I'm worried that when Milly said *nana*, Clara probably heard *Anna.* And I've realised that if anyone mentions that name, Clara gets furious and refuses to listen. Mum says that Anna is Clara's elder sister, and she'll have to see her at some point, but I've noticed Mum only says this to me, not Clara. When Priti suggested that Clara should meet Anna, Clara threw a mug of hot tea at her. Luckily it missed Priti, but poor Wilbur was terrified. He ran out of the kitchen as fast as a cat can run – which is pretty fast – and hid under my bed. We're meant to keep our bedroom doors closed, so Mum was a bit annoyed that I'd left mine open, which wasn't one hundred per cent fair. After all, it wasn't me who threw the tea. Also, my favourite mug got broken – the one which says "Though she be but little, she is fierce." It's an actual quote from Shakespeare, and we bought it in Stratford-upon-Avon, where he was born. Mum thought it was just right for me, even if I'm more middle-size than really little, and I'm not fierce at all. Clara's smaller and more fierce than me, to be honest.

Anyway, Mum and I are used to kids who sometimes shout and scream and throw things. It's stupid to get too attached to material things. But just in case, I've moved my other Shakespeare mug to my room. It's covered with insults like "cream-faced loon" and "loathsome toad". It'll be a great pen holder.

The doorbell goes. I jump up. "That'll be Adam," I say. I want to smuggle him upstairs so Mum doesn't see the extent of the makeover stuff that he's brought. And also because Adam and Mum don't always get on so well. It's not that they argue or anything, it's just a bit difficult, what with their past. Memories don't always go away just because you want them to.

Adam starts unpacking one of his bags in my bedroom, so Milly and I leave him there while we go and get his other bags. Then the doorbell rings again. I open the door. Lena's on the doorstep, smiling her fake grin.

"Hey, Ruby!" Lena says. "I heard you were having people over for makeovers!"

"Er, yes," I say, but I don't smile. I try to look as unwelcoming as I can.

Lena waves a packet of Hobnobs at me and says, "Here I am!"

There are two things I can do. I can say "You're not invited" and shut the door in her face. Or ...

"Oh, wow, great," I say. "Thanks, Lena." I take the biscuits and stand aside to let her in. "Hey, everyone, Lena's brought Hobnobs."

Milly joins me. "Oh, hi, Lena," she says. "I didn't really think you'd turn up. Wow, great – Hobnobs, my favourites!"

Oh. Great. That's why Lena is here. I should have guessed.

Milly's mum and Lena's mum met at pregnancy yoga, and their babies were born at the same hospital on the same day. The mums are still super best friends, so Milly has to spend an awful lot of time with Lena. In fact, their parents still think that Lena and Milly are best friends. I guess Milly doesn't feel she can tell the truth – that she can't stand Lena and her snarky, sneery sarcasm.

We get to my bedroom, and then I realise that Clara isn't there, so I rush down to get her. She's switched *Emmerdale* back on again.

"Come on, Clara," I say. "Adam's going to give us makeovers. And Mum's going out, aren't you?"

Mum sighs. "Well, I suppose so. If you're sure."

"Go to your Zumba class!" I tell her. "You deserve it!"

I can see that Clara doesn't understand, so I get Mum to demonstrate Zumba.

"It's my chance to escape to South America for an hour," Mum says as she sways her hips and waves her arms in the air. I swear that Clara's serious face lightens just for a minute. I switch the TV off again, and Clara follows me up the stairs.

Adam, Milly and Lena are in the bathroom already. Adam's washed Milly's hair and put in some foil highlights. Lena's begging him to cut her a fringe. As soon as she says it, I can see how it'll suit her – with that pointy chin, her swinging, shiny dark hair, those big brown eyes. She'll look fab.

Clara's shyer than shy. She won't even speak to Adam, but at least she doesn't leave, she just watches as he wraps Milly's hair in a towel and combs out Lena's. Clara seems fascinated. I suppose Adam is the first man (if you can call a seventeen-year-old a man) she's seen here. And he is interesting to look at, with his quiff that he's now dyed turquoise (he must have got bored with green), the diamond stud in his nose and his sharp contoured cheekbones. Adam is like a butterfly – our school uniform was his chrysalis, and he burst out of it as soon as he left school.

"What about you, Woman of Colour?" Adam asks, gently teasing me. "I brought some red colouring – it's really bright, I think it'd suit you. And I have some hair oil ..."

"No way," I say, covering my head. "I'm happy with it how it is ..."

"Yeah, yeah," Adam says. "And how about my Frida?"

"She's called Clara," I remind him. "Will you let Adam do your hair?" I ask her, but she shakes her head. But she seems happy to watch us. Maybe she'll change her mind.

"Do Milly and Lena first," I suggest. I bring in a chair from my bedroom for Lena to sit on, and Adam starts cutting her fringe. And cutting. And cutting. And …

"It's totally not straight!" Lena wails as she looks in the mirror. Her fringe is slanting over the upper bit of her forehead.

"No, well, not everything is …" Adam says. He's pulling a face, and I can't tell if he's smirking or actually really stressed. "Let me just have another go …"

"No, god!" Lena growls. "I look terrible! Don't even show me the back …"

It is a good thing he doesn't, as the back is a kind of zigzag.

"Oh my god!" Lena repeats. "I'm going to your salon tomorrow to complain! They need to sort this out before we go to school!"

"It's forty-five pounds for a senior stylist," Adam says. "You got me for free."

Lena bursts into tears. Milly gives her a hug.

"I'm getting out of here!" Lena says. "I should have known it'd be crap." She rushes out of the room, and Milly follows her.

Adam shrugs. "Are you feeling brave?" he asks Clara. "I'm not going to cut it, just style it. But it does need to be washed."

Clara shakes her head.

"Look, I *can* cut hair, you know," Adam insists. "I don't know why it went wrong with your friend, Ruby. Maybe because she kept tilting her head to one side."

"Clara, do you want to wash your hair yourself?" I ask, but she's backing out of the bathroom. We watch as she slips into her bedroom.

Milly and Lena are still downstairs, talking in angry hissing whispers.

"I'm so sorry!" Milly says. "I didn't know he'd screw it up!"

"I think Ruby got him to do it on purpose!" Lena tells her. "You know she doesn't like me!"

"Ruby wouldn't do that!" says Milly.

"She's obsessed with you! She won't let you have any other friends!"

"That's crazy!" Milly hisses. "Shut up, Lena!"

"You know it's true," Lena replies. "I'm an idiot. I should never have let that freak touch my hair."

Adam draws a breath. I pray he won't say anything. Then he starts packing his stuff into his bags. Downstairs, the front door slams behind Lena. Huh. Good riddance. I go downstairs and find Milly in the living room. I'm shocked to see that she's crying.

"Ignore Lena!" I say. "She wasn't even invited anyway."

"I invited her!" Milly says. "I thought it'd be fun – something we could all do together."

I don't know what to say.

"Now she's upset," Milly adds, "and her parents will be annoyed, and everyone will think it's my fault …"

"It's not your fault," I say, although privately I do think that Milly shouldn't be handing out invitations to other people's houses, even if it is her best friend. I mean her best friend's house. Lena certainly isn't her best friend.

I hear someone coming downstairs and the front door closing. Is it Clara? Or has Adam gone? I run downstairs, thinking, *What if Clara's running away?* But it's Adam, getting onto his bike.

"Where are you going?" I ask him. "What about Milly's hair?"

Adam shrugs. "You'll have to take the foils out. It'll be well cooked by now."

"Adam!" I shout. But he's gone, cycling fast down the road and not looking back.

Milly and I go into the bathroom, and I undo the foils and shampoo her hair. As I do it, I can see that something's gone badly wrong. She thought she was getting light honey-blonde streaks. But what she's got ... I wait until we've dried it ...

"Oh my god!" Milly cries. "Ginger chunks!"

"It's not so bad," I lie.

But Milly's not in the mood to be cheered up. "This is a disaster! This is a nightmare! And it's all your fault!"

"It's not my fault!" I argue. "It's Adam's!" But she storms out of the front door as well.

Huh. Great. My best friend hates me. Lena's going to make the most of it. And Clara never got her makeover at all.

I think about going into Clara's room and telling her what happened. I could get her advice and tell her how I really feel about Milly. How I feel about a lot of things. That I'm trying to sort out what's true and what's just a dream … trying to work out who I am.

That's what I'd do with a true sister. And I'm meant to treat Clara like she's part of our family.

I look at her door. I can hear a sound that might just be muffled crying. I really should go in and see if she's OK.

I take a deep breath, blink away my own tears and knock softly on her door.

"Clara?" I ask. "Are you all right?"

I open her door a tiny crack. She's sitting on the bed, her hands over her eyes, crying and crying. I go and get a box of tissues (Mum has loads in her bedside cupboard) and sit down on Clara's bed next to her.

"Here you are," I say. "Look … why don't you tell me what's bothering you? It might help."

Clara takes a tissue, rubs her eyes and tries to bring her sobs under control. There are a lot of shuddery hiccupping gulps before she gets some words out. But here they come.

"Go away!" Clara yells. "I hate you! I hate the witch too … and her cat! I want Mama! Why won't you let me see her?"

CHAPTER 7 / **Ruby**

Help me

As Clara yells at me, I'm so tempted just to walk out. But there's something about her, something so lonely and scared, that reminds me of some of the much younger kids that we've looked after. And I know that sometimes people say "go away" when they mean "help me".

So I sit down at the end of the bed and say, "It's not me that's stopping you seeing your mum. It's not Mum either. She's not a witch. And Wilbur's very sweet, and just wants to be friendly."

Clara stares at me like I'm speaking in Swedish.

I go on, "Mum's been asking the social workers when you can see your mum. We know it must be awful for you. We're here to help you, honestly."

It's working. She's gone very still, lying in her bed, staring at me.

"We're used to people coming here who are having a hard time," I say. "Little kids mostly. Shall I tell you about some of them?"

No response. But Clara's stopped crying, and her breathing sounds more even.

"Sometimes they've come from abroad," I tell her. "They're refugees. They arrive here with nothing – they've risked everything to come here. There was one boy, Hassan, he didn't speak any English. He used to wake up in the middle of the night, screaming. It took ages for him to tell us about Syria and what had happened to his family."

I'm not sure Clara even knows where Syria is, or why people might need to run away from there. She's so clueless about everyday stuff, how can she know about other countries?

"There's a war going on there," I explain. "Hassan's house was bombed. His aunty gave him money to try to escape." Talking about him is reminding me how much I miss Hassan. "He was so brave. He crossed the whole of Europe to get here. I think it really was helpful for Hassan to be here. He had food and a nice room, and us to talk to. And after a bit, when he'd learned some English, he did talk to us."

I pause. Will Clara take the hint? Will she talk to me? But she's still just lying down, those big eyes fixed on me. No sign that she wants to talk.

"You can make the room more personal if you want," I say. "Like, maybe the social worker could get you a photo of your mum? Or we have stuff. Mum keeps it in boxes ..."

Mum keeps everything. Toys, pictures, wall hangings. Things that kids can use to make their rooms feel more like home. She used to have a general "boy" box, with toy cars and animals, and a "girl" one, full of pink, sparkly stuff. Then she realised that was sexist, so she themed the boxes instead. An animal box. A space one. Transport. Fairies and magical creatures.

I mean, Clara's a bit old for most of it, but looking in them might give us an idea of what she likes. What she's interested in. Who she is.

"Anyway, what I'm trying to say is," I continue, "don't be angry with us. And if you tell me what we can do to help, then I can talk to Mum and we'll try – together ..."

"I'm scared ... Mama ..." Clara says, her words so soft I can't hear them all. Is she scared *for* her mum or scared *of* her?

"You shouldn't worry about her," I say. "She'll be getting better in the hospital."

"Where is the hospital?" Clara asks.

"I don't know which one she's in."

"Can you find out? Then I can go there ... find her ..."

I'm pretty sure that even if I could find out, I shouldn't be telling Clara. But there's no point in upsetting her more. I'm pretty proud of what a good job I'm doing in calming her down.

"I'll try," I say.

"Anna said there are cars that just come and take you wherever you want to go," Clara tells me.

This is the first time she's mentioned her sister without having a complete breakdown over it. Got to be progress, eh? She still manages to make taxis sound like magic carpets, mind you.

"Yes," I say. "But you need money, or an account ..."

"Oh."

"I've got books, too, if you're bored. And ..." I'm about to say my tablet, but I think better of it. She watches loads of TV as it is.

"I like books," Clara says.

At last! "OK, well there's a whole load in my room, and in the living room, or if you want we could go to the library. Actually, you'll like the library at school – or the LRC, they call it – the Learning Resource Centre. And the manager there, she's really nice too, and good at recommending books. And there's a reading club. I used to go to it."

Reading club was where I met Milly. She arrived with Lena, we bonded over a Louise Rennison book (*Withering Tights* – so funny) and that was it. I suggested she come along to drama group, and we became besties. We kept on going to reading club for a while, but then drama sort of took over with rehearsals and that.

"I think Lena still goes," I say to Clara. "You met her earlier. The one with the crooked fringe."

There's a tiny hint of a smile on Clara's serious face.

"She didn't like her hair," she says.

"No ..." I'm remembering how furious Milly was. How she blamed me. But she'll realise it was all Adam's fault ... won't she?

We look at my books, and Clara chooses one that I used to love when I was younger – *The Star of Kazan* by Eva Ibbotson. It's all about a girl searching for her mother, so maybe Clara will see something of her own story in there. Books are good for that. And the first box we pull out is the space one, and there's a wall-hanging covered in stars, which she loves, so we put it up in her room. "I used to watch the stars from my window," she tells me. "Before Mama blocked out the light."

I want to ask more questions, but Clara yawns. She's rubbing her eyes.

"Are you feeling a bit better now?" I ask. "You look like you need to sleep."

"I am." She sounds surprised. "Thank you ... Ruby. Thanks for saying you'll help me."

I'm pleased with myself. I really made a connection there. I broke past all that fury and strangeness.

Sometimes all you have to do is listen.

CHAPTER 8 / **Ruby**

Empirical evidence

The family-liaison officer at my school is called Mrs Kowalski, but she tells everyone to call her Mrs K. That's everyone who knows her, which isn't *everyone* – she's mostly there for people with special circumstances. Like Adam, and like Clara now, and like lots of people, actually.

She's in charge of the keys to the Vulnerable Toilet, which is just along the corridor from her small office tucked away behind the Learning Resource Centre. There are no windows in Mrs K's office, but the walls are covered with pictures. Some of them are photographs of flowers and animals and cities from around the world, and others have been drawn by kids – I guess people that she's helped at school. A whole load of pictures from a whole load of kids.

Mum went to see Mrs K to talk about Clara a couple of weeks ago, when she first arrived. Last week, Mum managed to persuade Clara to walk with her up the road to school to meet Mrs K. My instructions today are to deliver Clara to Mrs K before my first lesson starts. And I'd do it, but Clara walks so slowly. She is clearly really stressed by the noise and busy-ness of the kids crowding round the entrance and walking through the corridors. It means we get there five minutes late and I have to rush off to Geography.

That was hours ago, and now I'm in Science and the door has just opened and it's Mrs K and Clara.

My Science teacher, Mr Donnelly, pauses to say "Welcome, Clara", and he points at the empty desk in the front row. The desk just happens to be next to me, as Milly wasn't in first thing and she hasn't arrived yet. I hope she'll come in later – sometimes she does come in a bit late because of her anxiety issues. I hope she's not worrying about her hair and what people might say.

Lena is in school – she must have had an emergency haircut over the weekend, because now her fringe is even but super-short. Like, there's a massive gap between the fringe and her eyebrows.

I saw Lena trying to style it out as I walked through the playground earlier, but I couldn't say anything because of Clara. And anyway, what would I say?

Mr Donnelly is talking about stars. How they are formed from huge clouds of gas and dust that are pulled together by gravity in outer space. Then they get hotter and hotter until there's some nuclear reaction, and then they release energy and a star is born.

This makes me think about the old film called *A Star is Born*, with Barbra Streisand, which was my gran's favourite. It's all about a girl called Esther, who meets a man who's really famous as a singer. He helps her career, and then Esther does better than him and he kills himself. It's completely tragic. (Mum says that, as a feminist, it's not tragic at all, but I think she's missing the point. You can't bring politics into everything, especially films that were written in the olden days.)

And there's this bit where Esther says, "You can trash your life but you're not going to trash mine." I can never decide if Esther's right or she's a bit selfish to put herself first. But maybe that's how you get to be a star.

I realise that Mr Donnelly's asking me something, about red dwarves, I think, and I have no choice but to admit that I have no idea what he's talking about. It doesn't go down well. I try to focus for the rest of the lesson.

But it's hard because it's Drama next, and I don't know if Milly will show up for it, and whether she's still angry with me or not. I've been practising my audition speech, for Performance Academy, and I'm hoping that Ms Okafor will have time to hear it at break.

The bell rings. At last! I gather my stuff together, make for the door ... and then turn back. Clara's still just sitting there.

"Clara, where do you need to go next?" I ask.

She doesn't answer.

"Back to the LRC, I guess," Mr Donnelly says. "Mrs K likes to keep an eye on them for the first few weeks or so. Can you take her?"

"I can," I say. "Come on, Clara."

Clara seems reluctant to get up. She's still gazing at the whiteboard. "Mister ..." she begins.

"You can call him sir," I tell her. "Come on, I'm going to be late." The Drama studio is miles away from the LRC, and the Science block is even further. I sometimes think this school was designed by a very keen PE teacher.

Mr Donnelly must have a free period next, because he seems in no hurry. "What is it, Clara?" he asks.

"Those ... were you talking about ... stars? Like stars in the sky?" Clara says.

"That's right," Mr Donnelly says.

Clara's eyes are gleaming, I swear. Like she's going to cry.

"And how do you know all of that?" Clara asks.

"Well, different scientists build up knowledge from many experiments," Mr Donnelly explains. "They gather information, and they form theories and test them, until they are confident that they have found the true facts. That's called empirical evidence."

"But you said the stars are far away," Clara says.

It's nice to hear Clara getting chatty, it really is, after so much silence and tears, but the bell's gone already ...

"Don't worry, Ruby," Mr Donnelly says. "I'll walk Clara over to the LRC and maybe find her a book on space so she can do some reading before her next Science lesson. And we have Astrology Club, Clara, every Wednesday lunchtime. Ruby will bring you, won't you?"

"Yeah, yeah," I say. (Astrology Club? Yawn!) "Bye ... I'll come over at break, Clara. To check you're OK."

CHAPTER 9 / **Ruby**

A good argument

Of course, I'm late for Drama. And Ms Okafor isn't pleased. She's super-tough on punctuality. In fact, if I'd been any later she might have made me stay outside in the corridor.

"Thanks for joining us, Ruby," Ms Okafor says. "We're making groups of three or four. Hurry up and find some partners."

Milly is here at last – she's hard to miss, with those orange streaks – but she's already in a group with Lena and Katya and Sophie. They were all at primary school together. Milly's eyes look a bit pink. I try to smile at her, but she turns her back on me. I'm not sure if it's on purpose.

All the girls are in groups. I'm inching towards a three that includes Izzy from my tutor group, but then Mrs Okafor intervenes. "Come on, Ruby," she says, and her eyes sweep the room. "If you can't find a group … then join up with Eddie and Micah."

Brilliant. Micah's the one person in Year 11 who never grew out of making poo jokes. And Eddie's friendly, but he smells. I'm sorry, but it's true.

We have to improvise a family argument. Micah wants it to be about a blocked toilet.

"Oh, please!" I say. "That's stupid!"

"It's funny!" Micah argues.

"It's pathetic!" I tell him.

"What do you want it to be about, Ruby?" Eddie asks.

I realise that in our house, in my family, we're not very good at arguments. We're nice and reasonable about everything. The arguments only happen when foster kids do what Mum and the social workers call "acting out". They pick fights and shout and scream, and our job is to see beyond that – to find the scared, angry, upset person behind whatever the argument is about.

And if Dad and Kelly argue, they don't do it when I'm there at the weekends.

"Washing up?" I suggest, but I know it's a rubbish suggestion. "A kid who wants to stay out late?" I add.

"How about the mum is arguing with her boyfriend, and he gives her a smack, and the kid steps in to save his mum?" That's Eddie's suggestion.

I'm a bit taken aback. Is that what happens in his house? Poor Eddie. Maybe acting it out will help him. "Great idea," I say.

"You got that from *Hollyoaks*," Micah says.

All around us, people are starting their work. We're just standing around looking awkward.

"OK, so the toilet is blocked," Micah says. "You're the mum, Ruby, so you say, 'Who's blocked this toilet?! What the hell? What's this smell?'"

Eddie starts laughing and continues, "And then the dad comes along ... and he's holding his stomach, moaning and groaning ..."

Micah's face is creased up with laughing as he goes on. "And then the kid comes along too, and he starts ... you know ..."

I stuff my fingers in my ears to drown out Micah's loud farting noise.

"No way," I say. "We'll go with Eddie's idea."

"Ah, come on, Ruby," Eddie says. "It could be a laugh."

"Only for idiots like Micah," I say.

"All you have to do is be moany," Micah says to me. "Shouldn't be too difficult."

What? Does he mean that I'm moany? What is he talking about?

"No! I'm not doing it!" I tell him.

So we start working on Eddie's idea, but Micah keeps farting, and he and Eddie keep on giggling, and I know it's going to be rubbish. I don't even want to perform it when Ms Okafor claps her hands and says, "Right! Let's see how you've been getting on."

Izzy and her group act out a sad story about two sisters in love with the same guy. Then it's Milly's group's turn.

"It's called 'The Foster Sister'," announces Lena.

I gasp as they start, but I don't think anyone hears. OMG. There's a mum – played by Milly. She's so pleased with herself, so goody-goody, so fake-sweet to the foster kid (played by Katya, looking sulky, with her hair in stupid bunches). And then the sister. Played by Lena! She's so bossy and mean, pretending to be nice to her new sister, but actually it's all about making herself look good.

Do they mean me? Is that what they think I'm like? Does Milly think that?

People are laughing. They think it's good. Even Ms Okafor is nodding her head and smiling.

I start inching backwards. My eyes are stinging, and my throat feels sore and raw. No one's noticed, I think. No one apart from Eddie, and he doesn't count.

"We're going to make you look really good!" Lena, the mean sister, says. "Going to give you a makeover. Like Cinderella and her fairy godmother!"

Oh no. No, no, no.

"But it's not a fairy godmother ..." Lena adds. "Here he comes ..."

And, yes, here comes Sophie, doing a caricature of a gay man – acting over-the-top, camp, with lots of "ooh-errs". People used to do it to Adam a lot when he was at this school. Which was only last year. And kids in our class start to realise and nudge each other, and the smile on Ms Okafor's face fades away.

"That's all we've got time for," Ms Okafor says. "Girls, that was great until you strayed into pantomime land."

But the bell hasn't rung yet, so everyone hangs around and starts talking. I can hear people saying "Adam" and feel them looking at me, and Ms Okafor must be picking up on that too, because she goes over to Milly's group. I can see Ms Okafor shaking her head and Milly looking embarrassed. But Lena isn't even listening. She's looking at me, and her face is triumphant.

At last, the bell goes and I can escape. But Ms Okafor says, "Ruby, can you wait behind, please?" so I have to stand there while everyone files out.

At last it's just Ms Okafor and me. I wonder if she's going to say something about Adam, about me, but I'm not sure if she'll have made the connection. Not many people know he's my stepbrother.

"Everything all right, Ruby?" Ms Okafor asks.

"Yes," I say. I can't catch her eye.

"It's just that you didn't volunteer your group to perform to the class."

"It wasn't very good," I mutter.

"Improv is an important part of the audition process for the Performance Academy," Ms Okafor says. "You need to feel confident about it. Look at Milly and how she personified that awful woman. You can do that too, Ruby."

That awful woman. My cheeks are burning.

"And then there's your speech," Ms Okafor adds.

The speech for our auditions can come from a play or a film, or we can write it ourselves. I've been rehearsing two different ones – one of Juliet's from *Romeo and Juliet*, and a scene from *Titanic*.

"It's not coming across," Ms Okafor says. "It's not feeling real. Maybe you need something less mainstream."

"But …" I start.

"I think you should look for something else. Something that feels more like you."

"I don't want to feel like me." It comes out before I can stop myself. "I want to feel like someone else. That's the point of drama."

"I'm not saying it needs to be autobiographical," Ms Okafor says. "I'm saying it has to feel real. Take your emotions and channel them into the character you're playing."

I know she's saying sensible stuff. But all I'm hearing is:

You can't do it.

You're not good enough.

You're going to fail.

I just stand there looking as miserable as I feel, and Ms Okafor pats me on the arm and says she didn't mean to upset me.

"I'll have a think about your speech," she says. "Between us we can come up with the perfect choice."

I nod and try to smile. But I want to say, *Why bother, when it's clear I have no chance at all?*

CHAPTER 10 / Clara

More than magic

I never realised how much there was to know about the world!

And not just the world. The stars and the planets and the universe! Huge balls of fire, living and dying and burning – so far away from us that all we can see are twinkles of light.

My mind is growing every day to take in all this knowledge.

And every day I have delicious food to eat, and I sleep in a warm house and Lydia is nice to me.

Maybe she isn't a witch after all, even if she does have a black cat and her world seems like an enchantment. Ruby is kind too, and the cat pushes its face into my hand, asking to be stroked. It is soft and warm and it buzzes when it is happy.

There is so much more to life than magic and charms. There is Science. There is Maths. There are books and television and phones and computers.

At school, Mrs K is kind and patient. She teaches us about everything we need to know – about buses and trains and phones and shops. By "us" I mean me and there is a girl called Sadia and another one called Hadya. They come from a faraway land, where they had to hide away from danger. Like Mama said Anna and I had to. And Sadia and Hadya walked and walked to get here to England.

Like me, they didn't go to school. They were scared and hungry too. And now I can help them learn English and they are nice to me.

They are my friends.

I love school.

CHAPTER 11 / Ruby

How it all fits together

Clara's getting on fine. She's only doing four subjects – Maths, English, Science and History. She spends the rest of the time talking to Mrs K, or reading books in the library, or sometimes meeting with some of the other kids that Mrs K looks after. There are two girls in our year who are also new – asylum seekers from Afghanistan and Syria. Like Clara, they're completely clueless about basic general knowledge, so they have sessions with Mrs K where she teaches them about stuff – like getting around on trains and buses, and how the education system works, and anything else they want to know.

I was telling Adam about it at the weekend, and he said it was a Class for Aliens, which we thought was pretty funny because sometimes it feels as if Clara stepped out of a spaceship from another planet. Like when I showed her how her new phone worked, and how she could listen to music on it. Or when she tasted curry for the first time. Or when Adam and I took her to the cinema and she couldn't believe how big the screen was.

Because she's friends with Sadia and Hadya, she's sort of been accepted into a whole group of Afghani girls. It doesn't seem to matter that she doesn't speak their language, because some of them speak good English, so they translate for the others. And I see them sometimes at break and lunch, all hanging out together, and Clara seems quite at home. Even laughing.

So right now I feel as if Clara has more friends than I do. And she's happier at school than I am. And that's because when I talked to Milly about what happened in Drama – expecting her to apologise; blame Lena, feel sad for me – it all went horribly wrong.

I confronted them in the playground after school, when I'd moved from feeling tearful to being full of fury. I spotted Milly and went over. She was with Lena, of course, and Katya too.

"Oi!" I said. "How dare you take the piss out of my family?!"

"Did you think it was about you?" Lena replied with a smirk. "Isn't that a bit self-centred?"

"We didn't mean it like that ..." Milly said. "Ms Okafor told us to use material from real life." Milly's voice was all wobbly, like she was upset. What the hell did she have to be upset about? She wasn't the victim!

"You've got to admit that your family is a bit ... different," said Katya. "I mean, you're good material for a drama!"

"You have no right!" I shouted. "My family is my business!"

"Oh, get over yourself," Lena said. "You just can't bear that Milly has other friends."

"What?" I said. "No—"

"That's what this is about," Lena cut me off. "It's nothing to do with your weird family."

"But ... no—" I tried again.

"You don't even really like Milly," Lena said. "You *fancy* her."

"What?" I said. "Shut up!"

I mean, yes, I do fancy Milly. Anyone would.
And yes, I've never told her, because it's really
clear to me that she'd never be interested in a
relationship with a girl. She goes on about boys
all the time. And yes, I've never actually come
out, never told anyone I'm gay, because it seems
a bit pointless as I haven't got a girlfriend. I
can't imagine liking anyone as much as I like
Milly, so I probably never will. I'll just be single
for ever.

I'm pretty sure that things would be better
for me at Performance Academy. There's a
LGBT+ group. And if I don't get in ... well, there
will be somewhere else better than school, I'm
sure.

Anyway, Lena just stood there in the
playground, looking pleased with herself. Katya
and Sophie started giggling, and Milly didn't say
one word. We haven't spoken since, and I've
deleted all my social media accounts so I can't
see what they are saying about me.

I skipped Drama Club today just in case Milly
turned up. So instead I'm picking up Clara at
the LRC to walk home together. Sometimes she
finishes early, to avoid the crowds, and Mum

walks her home. But today Clara's stayed the whole day, and I'm grateful for her company to be honest. We hang around in the library for a bit, to let the crowds subside, and then start down the hill to home.

"How was your day?" I ask.

"I read about stars and planets and something called gravity," Clara says. "And Maths was enjoyable too."

Maths was enjoyable? Has anyone ever put those two words together?

"You actually like Maths?" I say.

"I'm not thinking about anything when I do it," Clara tells me. "No Mama or Anna, or anything difficult. Just numbers and puzzles and how it all fits together."

"Did you ever do Maths before?" I ask her.

"A bit. Sums in a book. Adding and taking away and multiplication. I always liked it. I wished I could do more. It's so clean and clear. Just right and wrong answers."

"And is that why you like Science too?" I ask.

Clara shakes her head and says, "I used to think everything was magical. But now I am learning that every single thing has a reason that can be explained. Every question. The world is put together in such a clever way, and I know nothing about any of it."

"Why not?" I say. The question bursts out of me. "Why didn't you go to school? How were you living? You can tell me, Clara."

She's changed so much in just a few weeks. She's even started to wear her hair loose. And now she nods and says, "It's OK. I don't mind telling you."

I'm just about to suggest that we take a detour by the High Street and go for a drink at the café, when I hear Clara gasp. A woman on the pavement opposite is shouting out and running into the road. Cars hoot and swerve. Somehow she doesn't get hit. And then she's there next to us, her arms wide open, saying, "Clara! Clara! It's me! It's Anna!"

CHAPTER 12 / Ruby

My little sister

Anna! She's got the same dark hair as Clara, but otherwise she couldn't be more different.

Anna must be twenty at least, and she's about a foot taller than Clara, which is partly because of her high-heeled boots. They add inches to her height and come all the way up her skinny jeans to her thighs.

Anna is wearing a tight black jumper and a red leather jacket. Her lipstick is a darker shade of red. Her dark eyes are lined with black eye pencil. It's like she's been drawn by an artist who only had three colours to use – black, white and red. And her long fingernails are dark red too, the colour of blood.

Clara doesn't look like she wants to be hugged, but she doesn't seem to be able to move away, and Anna throws her arms around her. She rocks Clara from side to side and says, "Clara! My little sister! It's really you!"

At last she lets go. Clara's so still, she's like a statue.

"I can't believe I found you!" Anna says. "I've been going to a different school every day, trying to see if I can find you as the kids go in and out. You're here! It's you." Anna strokes Clara's hair. "My little sister."

Clara's dropped her school bag. I pick it up for her. She's gone even paler than normal, and she's shaking. She doesn't seem to be able to say a word.

"Look," I say. "I'm not sure that Clara wants to talk to you. She's refused to meet you, hasn't she?"

Anna looks at me as if I'm a cockroach. "Who are you, her social worker?" she barks at me. "I've had enough of them interfering with her."

"I'm not a social worker," I reply.

Anna turns back to Clara and says, "Clara, we need to talk. You need to understand ... why I left. What's happened since then, and why I couldn't come back. It's been hard, but I've done so much. I've got a job and a place to live, and that can be your home too. You just have to talk to the police, darling. Tell them the truth."

"No ..." Clara's voice is very faint.

"You don't understand," Anna says. "You have to."

"You heard her," I say. "Leave Clara alone now. Or I'll call the police."

Anna looks like she's about to punch me, and I take a step backwards. Then she smiles and says, "Look, I can see that you think you're being kind to my sister, but you don't really understand her story ... our story ..."

"I understand enough to know that she's scared and unhappy," I say. "And that she doesn't want to see you. She says you're a liar."

Anna's eyes open wide. "I am not a liar! What are you talking about? Clara?"

Clara finds her voice at last: "You are a liar. You said ... you said you'd come back ..."

"I was going to—" Anna begins, but Clara cuts her off.

"You sent the men ..."

"I had to!"

"You made them take Mama away!" Clara yells.

"Clara, you couldn't live like that! I couldn't. You're at school now – you must realise what was happening to us ..."

Clara's standing there crying, and I can't bear it.

"Go away!" I shout. "Can't you see what you're doing? Go away!"

"Who even are you?" Anna says. Her voice is so cold it makes me shiver. "Look, I can see you think you've got Clara's best interests at heart. You've met her at school, and you've made a friend, and I'm grateful to you for that. She needs friends. She's been so lonely. But I'm here, and I'm not going to hurt her. So if you can just leave us alone, we'll be fine, won't we, Clara?"

"I'm Ruby," I say. "And I'm Clara's sister now. And there's no way I'm leaving her alone with you."

CHAPTER 13 / Ruby

The rest of us

Anna won't give up. It feels like hours that she spends trying to persuade Clara to come with her, to talk, to listen, to understand.

In the end, Anna scribbles her address and phone number on a scrap of paper and thrusts it at Clara. "Call me," Anna says. "Or come and find me, any time. Please, please do it. I can't bear this."

Clara takes the paper, puts it into her pocket.

"OK. I'll see you again. Call me," Anna says again.

"Just leave her alone now," I tell Anna. "She's had enough. Can't you see?"

We stand and watch as Anna walks away. It's getting dark now, and Clara looks exhausted, so

I hail the next bus that goes past and we sit on it until we reach the end of our street.

As we walk to our house, I ask Clara, "Are you OK? Do you want to … you said you'd tell me your story …"

But Clara just shakes her head. When we get home, she tells Mum she's got a headache and doesn't want any supper. I hear her bedroom door close, and I feel left out. I mean, I get that it was really upsetting and all that, but I stood up for her, and I don't even know what's going on.

I don't tell Mum about Anna. She'd only ring Priti and there would be a big fuss, and I can see that Clara would hate that. She's promised to tell me her story. I'll hear all about Anna then. While I'm waiting for supper, I try to find a piece for my audition. I read through a few speeches. But nothing feels real to me. There's nothing that I can connect to. It doesn't help that I can imagine Milly doing them all so much better than me. If you're tall and thin and beautiful, then every playwright in the world wants to write for you. That's how it seems to me.

What about the rest of us? The ones who look and feel different? Where are the speeches for us?

Who tells our story?

"Tell me about school," Mum says as she serves up our supper. "How's the drama group?"

"We're not really doing much at the moment," I tell her. "Not since the performance."

"How's the audition prep going? Do you want me to hear you rehearse?"

I shrug and say, "I think it's mostly decided on improv on the day. I don't think I've got much of a chance really."

"It's not like you to be defeatist, Ruby," Mum says. "Think positive!"

"I am thinking positive," I lie. "But I have to be realistic."

"You can only do your best. Do you think I should take some food up to Clara? She didn't look well, poor little scrap. I hope she's not sickening for something."

"I think she's just tired," I say. "She seemed OK when we left school."

"I'll just go and check," Mum says.

I should tell Mum about Anna. I know I should. But then Mum would have to call Priti, and there'd be all sorts of questions, and Clara would feel even worse. Somehow I don't want to interfere. Maybe it's none of my business. I keep on thinking about Lena's performance of the foster sister, the one who turned everything to her own advantage. Was that meant to be me? Do people know me better than I know myself?

Am I the sort of person who uses other people? Did I really cut Milly off from her other friends? But if that was true … why would she let me do that?

When I think back to when we first met, all I can remember is how much Milly and I liked each other. And how brilliant it was to have a friend like that. It was irritating that Lena and Katya and the others all wanted to intrude on the time Milly and I spent together. After all, they didn't have so much in common with Milly. Just the past.

Mum's back. "Clara's asleep. I suppose school tires her out."

"She likes school," I say. I'm hoping Mum will ask if I like school too, so I can tell her that I don't any more. In fact, I'd like to leave. But Mum's obsessed with Clara.

"That's so wonderful!" Mum says. "I'm so happy! The police want to talk to her again, you know. She wouldn't say anything before."

I should tell Mum about Anna now. I really should. "What do they want to talk to her about?" I ask.

"They want to ask Clara about her home life." Mum lowers her voice. "Priti told me a bit. Her mother is in a psychiatric hospital. They think she neglected her daughters. They think she tried to cut them off from the outside world. The older sister got out and told the authorities."

"Mum—" I start.

But the doorbell rings before I can tell her about Anna. Mum goes to answer it.

A minute later she's back.

"It's for you," Mum says. "It's Milly."

CHAPTER 14 / Ruby

Melting into shadows

Milly is standing there on our doorstep, her hair shining in the beam of the security light. Her orange highlights have faded, or been re-done, and now she's all golden and glowing.

"What do you want?" I ask. I'm just being cautious, but it comes out all wrong. An aggressive bark, not a nervous question.

"I need to talk to you," Milly says. "I hate that we're arguing like this."

What?

"Look, it wasn't me that started it!" I say. "It was all you! You blamed me for your hair ... and you blanked me at school. And then that drama lesson ..." I can't go on.

"I feel awful about that!" Milly says.

"Good! So you should."

It's freezing, and we're both shivering.

"Can I come in?" Milly asks.

I'm about to say "OK, come in then" when I feel something head-butt my leg. Wilbur! He's not meant to go out of the front door, but he dodges around me and shoots past Milly into the darkness.

"Wilbur!" I wail. "He's not meant to go out of the front! He could get run over!"

"What's happening?" Mum calls.

"It's Wilbur," I call back. "He's run out of the front door! I'm going to look for him."

It's very hard looking for a black cat in the dark. You think you see him, and then you realise that it's a clump of flowers or a food waste bin. Wilbur can melt into shadows, lurk in corners, just close his eyes and vanish.

Milly and I walk up and down the street, looking and calling.

"Look, the drama thing, it was a mistake," Milly says. "I didn't mean it to happen like that."

"You made fun of my mum in front of everyone," I reply. "And Lena made fun of me, and as for Adam …"

"Lena did that!" Milly says. "She made it like that! It wasn't meant to be making fun, it was a way … I was trying to make Lena understand your family more …" Milly tries to explain.

"You were what?" I ask.

"I thought … if she understood you … if she thought about what your life is like …"

"Like my life needs so much understanding!" I say. "Thanks a lot, Milly!"

"People like Lena, they don't understand," Milly says. "They don't get that not everyone lives in a house with their mum and dad and brother. They're stuck in a box. Lena thinks—"

I interrupt. "She thinks I'm weird and strange because my parents are divorced? Because Mum fosters kids? Because my stepbrother has blue hair and isn't really qualified as a hairdresser? Or maybe she doesn't like it that my dad's parents came from Jamaica?"

"She thinks you don't like her," Milly says.

"Well, she'd be correct."

"But, you know, she thinks you didn't want to be her friend," Milly explains. "When we first got to know you. She liked you, Ruby, but you froze her out."

"I didn't freeze her out! I don't even remember ..."

And that's it. I don't remember thinking about Lena at all. I was dazzled by everything about Milly, and I wanted to be her friend. I just saw Lena as a whiny, insecure, annoying obstacle in my way. She'd had Milly as her friend for far too long, I thought, and besides, Lena had two other really good friends. She could make do with them. I wanted Milly for myself.

"I feel caught in the middle," Milly says. "I have for ages. So I thought ... if we did a drama thing about a foster family, Lena might understand you more. And you'd see that. And it would sort of bring everyone closer together. But it didn't work out like that, and I got all flustered, and it all went badly wrong."

"But when we talked, you said it was a joke," I say. "And when Lena said ... when she said that I ..." I can't get the words "fancied you" out of my mouth.

"I know, I ..." Milly is struggling too.

"You just stood there," I say. "You didn't say anything!"

"I didn't know what to say," Milly replies. "I was so embarrassed! Of course you don't fancy me! Why would you, with this stupid ginger hair?"

Eh?

"There's nothing wrong with your hair," I say.

"I'm so awkward and ginger and freckly ..." Milly says. "No one's ever going to fancy me."

"Well, hang on ..." I say. Should I tell her now? What should I do?

She's going to spoil it, I know. She's going to say something like, "Well, Robert will never look at me." Robert is the sixth-former that all the girls like because he's fit and nice and funny, and you can't ask much more of a seventeen-year-old boy it seems.

But Milly doesn't say that. She says, "Ruby, tell me the truth. Are you gay?"

I hesitate. Can I trust her? Or is this all some trick inspired by Lena?

And then Wilbur appears in the light of a street lamp, and I gallop up the road to catch him. The moment's lost.

CHAPTER 15 / Ruby

Lost

In the morning I sleep late, and when I get up, Mum's looking happy.

"Clara's gone out to meet some friends," Mum says. "Sadia and Hadya? She said they were going to Top Shop."

"Really?" I say. "Wow."

"I know, it's so nice to see how she's settled down. What a difference."

I can't really imagine Clara doing this, but you never know. And then I remember Anna writing down her address and phone number and pushing it at Clara. And Clara hadn't crumpled it up or dropped it on the pavement. She'd put it in her pocket.

Has Clara gone off to meet her sister? But why would she, as she refused to before? Maybe she'd run away from her sister instead.

I should tell Mum now. But if I tell her, then she'll have to tell Priti and the police, and I'll look stupid. And it might reflect on Mum's ability to be a good foster parent. And if she couldn't be a foster parent any more, then she'd be lost, she'd be broken and it'd be my fault.

"All ready to go to Dad's?" Mum asks.

"Oh …" I say. "I'd better go and pack my bag."

I can't decide what to do. I try calling Clara's phone, but there's no reply. And when I get to Dad's I keep trying all morning while I'm chatting with Kelly and playing with Freya and telling Dad about school – missing out all the important stuff, as usual.

It's not that I want to have secrets. It's just that it's so much easier to babble on about French and History and my nightmare English teacher than saying stuff like, "By the way, Dad, I'm a lesbian, but I don't think it's something you have to worry about as no one's ever going to want to go out with me." Or, "Actually, my best friend and I are having the worst time communicating, and I don't know what to do because I'm madly in love with her." Or, "I want to be an actress more than anything in the world, but I'm going to mess up my audition because I'm so crap."

Or even, "Should I tell Mum about Clara's real sister?"

It's kind of exhausting, and I'm grateful for Freya, who just wants me to make farm animal noises and put cows in and out of a wooden shed. She's sort of obsessed with cows at the moment.

Anyway, while Freya and I are mooing at each other, I'm checking my phone. Maybe Clara will see that I've called and messaged her, and will respond – but would she do that? A few weeks ago, Clara didn't even know what phones were.

Dad and Kelly take Freya out in her buggy, and I say I've got homework to do. Five minutes after they've gone, Adam comes in.

"Hey, sis," he says. "How's it going?"

"Oh … OK," I reply. "How about you?"

Adam pulls a face and says, "I got sacked."

"You got sacked? Why?"

"Overslept too often," Adam explains. "Plus I was rubbish at sweeping up. Plus the boss thought I was snarky. Plus your mate's mum complained that I'd chopped her daughter's fringe and demanded a free restyle. And when the boss said no, because I wasn't trained and I didn't cut her fringe at the salon, she said she'd slag us off on social media. So Ellie-Mae did it for free and then took the money off my wages. So I wasn't her favourite person anyway, even before today's disaster."

"What was today's disaster?" I ask.

"Handed Ellie-Mae air freshener when she asked for hairspray. The client had an asthma attack."

"Oh, Adam."

I like Adam so much when he's not trying to score points off other people by being funny.

He sits down at the table with me.

"You don't look your normal happy self," Adam says.

I shake my head.

"What's up?" he asks.

It's so easy once you start. I open my mouth and it all comes out – Milly and Lena and Ms Okafor and Clara and everything. And I feel so much better, just telling someone everything that's been going on.

And Adam doesn't say anything snarky or mean, just encouraging stuff like, "Sounds like Milly really loves you, but you just have to trust her with the truth." And, "I've seen you act and you're really good. But having low self-esteem is a total sucker."

After I've finished, Adam says, "I can't believe you haven't told me this before. We could have been our own little LGBT+ support group."

"I'm sorry," I say. "I suppose I didn't feel we were close enough."

"Not really family, eh?"

"It wasn't that," I say, but then I add, to continue being truthful, "well, sort of. I spent a long time resenting you, thinking it was because of you that Mum and Dad spilt up."

"Not my fault," Adam says.

"I know. It wasn't fair of me. And then people were mean to you at school, and I didn't want them to do that to me as well …"

"But we weren't always at school."

"I know," I say, "but I was thinking about me, not you. Sorry. And I thought you were sort of sarcastic, and you didn't like me or my mum."

"I just felt awkward and bad," Adam explains. "Because it did feel like my fault that your dad and my mum … I mean, they'd never even have met if it wasn't for me. Your dad was a brilliant mentor. It pissed me off when he and mum fell for each other, if that helps. And I really could have done without moving schools. Not that I liked my old school any better."

"I always thought you didn't like us because of the house," I say. "I mean, if Mum and Dad had sold it, you could all be living somewhere bigger. But Mum needed the extra bedrooms to keep fostering."

Adam shrugs and says, "It's just a bit cramped because of Freya. But she's great. And

I'll get out of here one day. Just as soon as I work out what I want to do with my life."

"Not hair?" I ask.

"I'm thinking about going to college," Adam says. "Maybe have a go at A levels. Try to get my Maths GCSE," he adds.

"I might do that," I say. "If I don't get into Performance Academy."

"You will get in," Adam tells me. "You're ace. You just have to find the right speech."

It's 4 p.m. and Dad and Kelly are back. Dad overhears the last bit and asks, "What do you mean, the right speech?"

I explain, "Ms Okafor thinks the one I'd picked isn't right for me. But nothing seems to be. I mean, I'm not exactly the heroine type."

"Rubbish!" Dad slaps the table. "You take a look, and you'll find something that's just right for you. You know, Ruby, you've had a lot of interesting experiences that most people your age haven't had. You've met lots of people. Take all of that, and see how you can build on it. Does your mum know you're worrying about the audition?"

"Well ..." I say. "Sort of ..."

"Will you tell her?" Dad asks.

"Yeah. I will. Actually, I need to call her."

I go into the bedroom to give Mum a call.

"Is Clara back?" I ask Mum over the phone. "It's just that – I should have told you – I'm a bit worried about her. We bumped into her sister yesterday and—"

"Don't worry," Mum says. "Clara's here and so is Anna, and everything's going well."

CHAPTER 16 / Clara

My sister

Sadia and Hadya and I are in a shop full of beautiful clothes. Dresses with embroidered flowers, woollen scarves in blues and greens and purples, shiny coats and soft velvet robes. We touch and point and feel them, holding jewels to our ears, laughing and smiling. Like sisters. Like friends.

It doesn't matter that we can't speak each other's language. We are learning all the time.

And I think about Anna. How she would feed me and dress me when I was small.

How Anna would hold me tight in the days before the man left. In the days when he would shout and hit Mama, again and again.

How Anna would say, "Mama's ill. She's scared of everything! But the world isn't something to be scared of."

How Anna would say, "This is all wrong! We should be at school! She's keeping us prisoner!"

But then Anna went away. She left me. She vanished.

And I loved Mama so much that when she told me Anna was bad and evil and a liar, I believed her.

Because Anna had gone away and left us. And then Anna had told the police bad things.

But now I am thinking more and more.

Anna wanted me to go to school.

Anna knew Mama was ill.

Anna knew the world had wonderful things in it. She knew it was beautiful. And when I saw her, she looked so pretty, with her golden earrings and her shiny red coat. Not like the thin, sad, angry Anna I remember.

So in the clothes shop I tell Sadia and Hadya that I am going – I wave my hands to say goodbye, and then we all say, "See you tomorrow."

And I call Lydia on my phone. "I need to see my sister," I tell her. "I have her number. Can you call her?"

CHAPTER 17 / Ruby

The truth is complicated

I get Dad to drive me back to Mum's. I can't help myself. I want to know what's going on.

Anna looks different today. She hasn't got all that harsh make-up on, and she's just wearing leggings and a pale-blue shirt. It makes her look younger and softer, and a lot more like Clara.

Mum and Clara and Anna are drinking tea, and there's a chocolate cake, and they're all smiling.

"It's all right," Clara says as soon as I come in. "Anna and I couldn't find the right way to talk to each other yesterday, but it's better now."

Anna wipes her eyes and says, "Sometimes, when you love someone a lot, it all comes out wrong."

"What happened?" I ask. I can hardly believe what I'm hearing.

"Clara came back from the shops about an hour after you left," Mum tells me. "She told me about meeting Anna. And a lot of other things as well. I suggested that we invite Anna here, for tea. So we called her, and then we made a cake, and here Anna is."

"I'm sorry, Ruby," Clara says to me. "I wished you were here. You and Lydia, and Wilbur too – you helped me so much. It made me see that Anna was right."

"What do you mean?" I say, with my mouth full of cake.

Anna takes over. "Our mother, she wasn't well. She started acting strange, as if the whole world was against her. At first, when I went to school, she'd just do things like make me wash all over as soon as I came home. Then she didn't send Clara to school at all. And gradually ... bit by bit ... our mother just withdrew. She didn't trust anyone at all."

"She was scared," Clara adds. "She was scared of men. And germs. And the world."

"Your social workers say that they think your mum was abused in the past," Mum says. "She probably couldn't bring herself to tell you. I'm sure she thought she was doing the right thing."

Anna says, "It wasn't right. Poor Clara, she knew nothing at all about the world. It was abuse. I was the bad girl – I would escape, go and find out what the world was like. It made our mother ... well—"

"Upset," Clara says, at the exact same time Anna says, "Violent."

It makes me think the truth is so complicated. It's like a diamond with many sides.

"I had to leave," Anna continues. "And when I did, after I'd found a job and a place to live, I went back. I said that Clara should come and live with me. But our mother wouldn't allow it. It made her even worse. She stopped going out at all. She nailed a piece of wood over the letter box. I don't know what you were living on ..."

"Macaroni," Clara says. "Porridge. Sometimes rice."

"I told the police," Anna says. "I had to. And they raided the house."

"They decided that Anna and Clara's mum needed help," Mum says. "We've had to wait, to see what would happen with your mum. Poor Clara, you've missed her so much. But we've just heard that they've decided not to prosecute her – there's no point ..."

"Mama needs help and love," Clara says. "I know Anna's angry with her, but I can't be."

"I'm angry for you!" Anna says.

"Please don't be," Clara tells her.

"So, what's going to happen?" I ask. "Is Clara going to stay with us? Or are you going to live with Anna?"

We're all looking at Clara, but she's got her head down, stroking Wilbur, who's keeping her feet warm. Wilbur only does that to people he likes.

Mum says, "I've been talking to Priti. They'll let you stay with us as long as you need to, Clara. Anna can visit, and we'll take you to see your mum in hospital."

Clara's voice is muffled but clear enough to hear. "I'd like that."

CHAPTER 18 / Ruby

The moment of truth

"You know what?" I say to Milly. "I need your help."

It's been a week since our awkward, unfinished conversation on the doorstep, and I haven't found a way to talk to Milly yet. Perhaps I never will. But we're both in the LRC at school (did she follow me in here?), and we're almost the only ones here. It's now or never.

After all, what have I got to lose?

"How can I help?" Milly asks. She's smiling. God, she's so gorgeous.

"I need to find an audition speech," I say. "Something that's right for me. Something that's about someone who gets things wrong ... who tries to do her best but ends up upsetting people ..."

"Oh," Milly says. "Well, isn't that just about everyone?"

"True. Well, ideally, the speech would be about someone who never feels they really fit in. Who worries about what people are going to think. Who keeps secrets because it's easier that way."

"I'm a bit like that," Milly says. "Like, there's stuff I never even told my best friend."

"Your best friend?" I ask. "Do you mean your oldest friend? Or maybe *one* of your best friends?"

"No," Milly says. "My best friend."

The only other person in the LRC, a sixth-former who's been working at a computer, switches off his monitor. He picks up his bag and says, "You two OK to switch off the lights when you're done?"

"Oh, yes, fine," I say.

"No problem," Milly says.

He leaves. The door swings behind him. And this is it. The moment of truth.

"I'm really looking for a speech by a contemporary lesbian playwright," I say. "Actually, I may never have mentioned it, but that sort of thing reflects who I am. Not all of who I am, but just an important bit."

"I wish you'd said," Milly tells me.

"I just did."

There's a moment – just a moment – where I think it's all going to be perfect. That Milly's going to lean forward and kiss me, and we realise it's all been one giant misunderstanding and we get our perfect happy-ever-after. The ultimate reward for telling the truth.

But it's not quite like that. Milly and I look at each other and we smile, and I feel all the excitement bubbling up inside me. Then she says, "I'm pretty sure I can't be who you want me to be, but I really love you anyway."

"That's OK," I say automatically. The excited bubbles die down, and I feel like an idiot and a fool.

But then Milly grabs my hand and says, "It'll be OK. Whatever happens, we've got a brilliant friendship. Best friends for ever and ever, OK? True sisters?"

And I feel like it's going to be all right.

CHAPTER 19 / Ruby

This is how it feels

You're allowed to take one person in with you when you audition. Mum and Dad offer, of course, and so does Ms Okafor, but I pick Adam.

I let Adam do my hair and pick my clothes. And I really like the red colour he dyes my curls. My hair springs out from my head like a setting sun. I look fierce. Small but fierce.

And the clothes work too – simple black jeans and top.

It was Adam's idea to give up the hunt for a speech and for me to write my own stuff instead. And he said I shouldn't worry too much about telling my own story. "It'll come out in everything you do anyway," Adam told me. "You won't be able to help yourself."

Adam suggested interviewing Clara. Finding out as much as we can about her story. And then writing it up as a monologue. Adding more details. Playing with the facts until it makes something that is its own truth. Its own story.

And now it's just me and the panel from the academy, and I feel quite calm and confident. If this chance doesn't work out, another will come. I just have to be strong and patient. I have to believe in myself.

I open my mouth and begin to speak.

"This is how it feels when they raid your house ..."

CHAPTER 20 / Clara

True sisters

This is how it feels when your life is happy.

Mama is getting better. Anna and I visited her. She was very weak and very sleepy, but she was able to hug us and beg for our forgiveness and tell us that she was improving. It will take a long time. She may never be completely well. But it was enough.

And I see Anna all the time, but I live still with Lydia and Ruby. And Wilbur, the nicest cat in the world.

We are having a party for Ruby, to celebrate her getting in to her new school. She is going to learn to be an actress, and she is so excited. Ruby and Milly are going together. Ruby cried when she heard the news.

The party is a surprise, so Milly is keeping Ruby away from the house while we get it ready. Ruby's mum and dad, her sister Freya, Adam and me. We've made cakes, which smell of cinnamon and toffee, and we've trickled icing onto ginger biscuits. There are bowls of olives and drinks that fizz, and Lydia's put pizzas in the oven. Pizza is my favourite food now, I think. Or maybe cold, creamy ice cream.

Ruby looks different now she knows she has a place at the school where she wants to go. Her back is straighter. Her eyes are brighter. She is happy and strong, and she sings a lot. It makes me happy to hear her.

Adam has put stuff on my hair to make it shiny, and twisted it up at the back and put flowers on the top of my head. He says I look like someone called Frida and showed me a picture of her. I like how she looks – like a brave, strong person. That is the person I want to be. I am not a scared mouse any more. I am going to learn Maths and Science, and find out more and more about the world.

I love the flowers and the trees, the feel of sunshine and wind on my skin. I love the way Wilbur purrs, and my new dress (such a deep, rich red colour). I love the music of Bach and Ariana Grande and Madonna. I love hot chocolate, and I am learning to swim, and last weekend Anna and I caught a train to Brighton and I saw the sea.

Ruby bought me a mug of my own. It says on it "Though she be but little, she is fierce". I love these words, and I love my mug. Ruby's not my real sister, but she cares as if she is. She understands me. She sees the true Clara – she sees what I can be.

We are true sisters. Ruby and me, Anna and me. And Hadya and Sadia as well. We support each other. We love each other. We have fun together. I am so lucky to have them.

We hear the sound of a key in the door. Here she comes.

Ruby, shining like a jewel.

Acknowledgements

Thank you to all at Highgate Wood School, especially the wonderful Kate and Noa in the LRC and Miss Meltem, the Family Liaison Officer. And thank you to the Ruby Rose Cafe in Crouch End, where much of this book was written. Special thanks to Liz Kessler. Much love to my truly amazing sister Deborah and all my other True Sisters. You know who you are.

Our books are tested
for children and young people by
children and young people.

Thanks to everyone who consulted on
a manuscript for their time and effort in
helping us to make our books better
for our readers.